Blue's Clues

Something to Say

Published by Advance Publishers, L.C.
www.advance-publishers.com

©2000 Viacom International Inc. All rights reserved. Nickelodeon,
Blue's Clues and all related titles, logos and characters are trademarks
of Viacom International Inc.
Visit Blue's Clues online at www.nickjr.com

Written by Ronald Kidd
Art layout by J.J. Smith-Moore
Art composition by Brad McMahon
Produced by Bumpy Slide Books

ISBN: 1-57973-074-4

Blue's Clues Discovery Series

Hi, there! Blue, Magenta, and I are about to go for a walk. Would you like to come along? Great!

What's wrong, Blue? You hear someone crying? So do I! I think it's coming from the kitchen. Let's check it out before we leave.

It's Paprika! I wonder why she's crying.

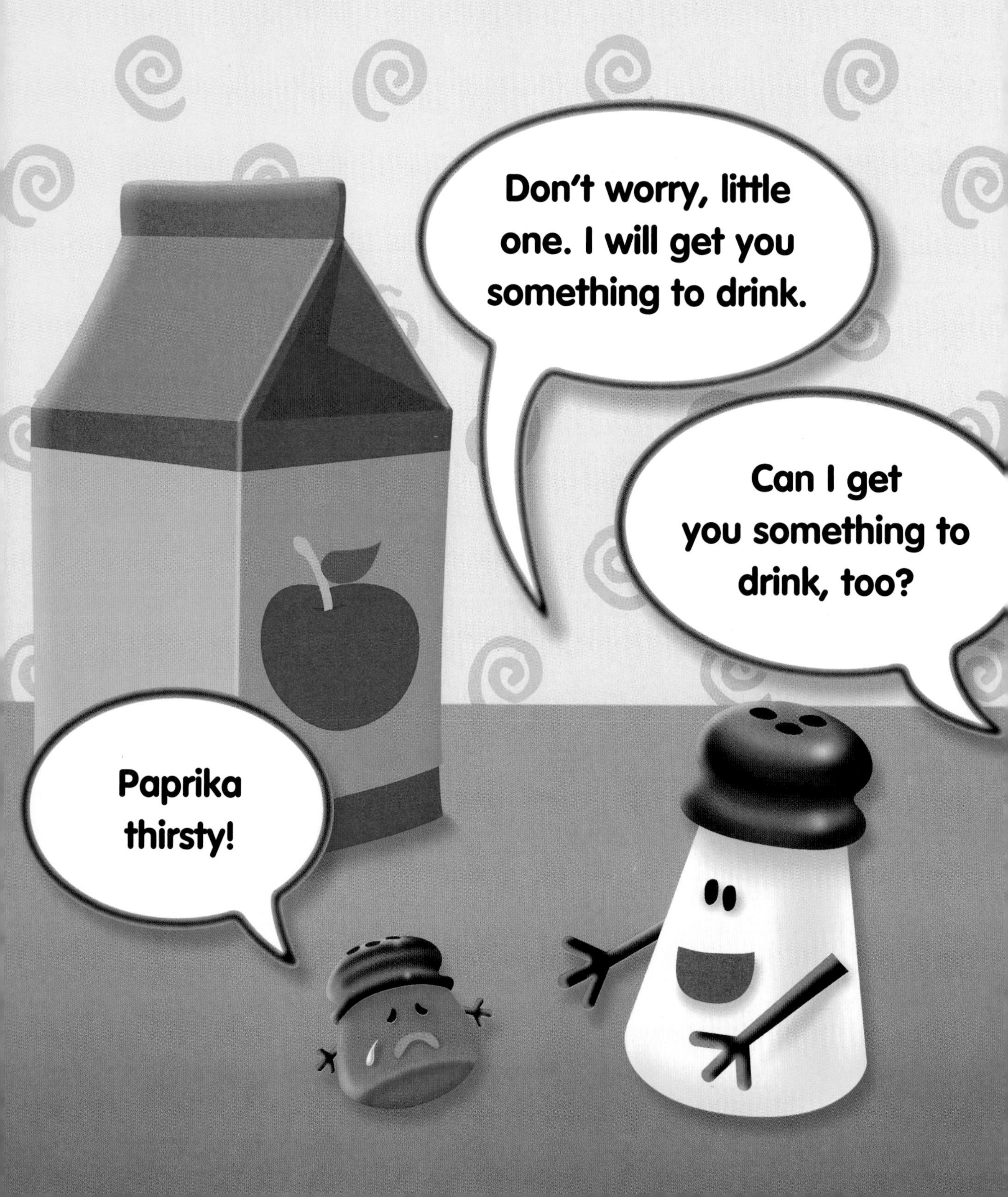

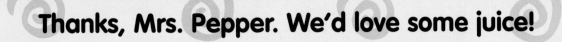
Thanks, Mrs. Pepper. We'd love some juice!

Before Paprika could talk, she communicated to us by making sounds and crying.
Yes, but now that she uses words, it's even easier to understand what she wants.

Blue, you have a new way to communicate?
What is it? Oh! You want us to play Blue's Clues
to figure out a new way to communicate!
Will you help us? You will? Great!

You see a clue already? Oh, it's the paper cup for my juice! Our first clue is a paper cup!

Hey, maybe we'll find more clues on our walk. Let's go!

'Bye, Paprika! So long, Mr. Salt and Mrs. Pepper! Thanks for the juice!

Oh, look! A vegetable garden. I wonder what they're growing.

Hey, those must be pictures of all the vegetables growing in the garden—carrots, cabbage, tomatoes, and corn.

I guess that pictures are another way to communicate. Huh. I never thought of that before.

Hey, I wonder what this string is for. Do you know? Yeah! Good thinking! The string must be here so no one will step on the new plants. That was a smart thing to do. You think so, too?

Oh! You see a clue! String is our second clue! So what could Blue's new way to communicate be using a paper cup and string? I don't know either. I guess we'll have to find our third clue.

What's this? Oh, yeah! A stop sign!
Hey, it looks like signs are a good way to
communicate, too. Right! The garden used
picture signs, and this is a word sign. Cool!

It looks like Blue is trying to tell us something.
What do you think she wants us to do? Yeah! Go
to the park. Let's go!

Wow! Listen to all that! I wonder where all of those different sounds are coming from. Do you know?

Ah . . . the frogs, birds, and squirrels must be making those sounds. That must be how they communicate with each other. That's pretty cool!

What's that? You see a clue? Oh! Another paper cup. Great! Our third clue is a paper cup. Hey, we have all three clues!

You know what that means, don't you? We'd better go home to our . . . Thinking Chair!

Hmmm. So what could Blue's new way to communicate be using two paper cups and a piece of string?

Do you think maybe it's drinking juice together? No, I guess not. Hmmm. I wonder what it could be. Do you know?

That's it! A paper cup telephone! When you stretch a string between two paper cups, you can talk to someone.

We just figured out Blue's Clues!

Blue! We sure are lucky to have such smart friends, aren't we?
Thanks for all your help! 'Bye!

BLUE'S PAPER CUP TELEPHONE

You will need: a pen, two paper cups, and a piece of string

1. Ask a grown-up to poke a small hole in the center of the bottom of each cup with a pen.

2. Feed one end of the string through one cup bottom, and the other end of the string through the other cup bottom, so that the two cup bottoms are facing each other.

3. Tie a knot at each end of the string.

4. Keep one cup and give the other cup to a friend. Then move away from each other until the string is stretched tight.

5. Talk into your cup while your friend listens at the other cup. Then you listen while your friend talks.